sleepoverclub
.com

by Narinder Dhami

An imprint of HarperCollinsPublishers

Northamptonshire Libraries & Information Service

Peters	31-Jan-02
CF	£3.99

The Sleepover Club ® is a
registered trademark of HarperCollins*Publishers* Ltd

First published in Great Britain by Collins in 2001
Collins is an imprint of HarperCollins*Publishers* Ltd
77-85 Fulham Palace Road, Hammersmith,
London, W6 8JB

The HarperCollins website address is
www.**fire**and**water**.com

1 3 5 7 9 8 6 4 2

Text copyright © Narinder Dhami 2001

Original series characters, plotlines
and settings © Rose Impey 1997

ISBN 0 00711733 7

The author asserts the moral right to
be identified as the author of the work.

Printed and bound in Great Britain by
Omnia Books Limited, Glasgow

Conditions of Sale
This book is sold subject to the condition
that it shall not, by way of trade or otherwise,
be lent, re-sold, hired out or otherwise circulated
without the publisher's prior consent in any form,
binding or cover other than that in which it is
published and without a similar condition
including this condition being imposed
on the subsequent purchaser.

Sleepover Kit List

1. Sleeping bag
2. Pillow
3. Pyjamas or a nightdress
4. Slippers
5. Toothbrush, toothpaste, soap etc
6. Towel
7. Teddy
8. A creepy story
9. Food for a midnight feast:
    chocolate, crisps, sweets, biscuits.
    In fact anything you like to eat.
10. Torch
11. Hairbrush
12. Hair things like a bobble or hairband,
    if you need them
13. Clean knickers and socks
14. Change of clothes for the next day
15. Sleepover diary and membership card

Spooky Stories   Music   Shopping   Midnight Feast   Games

CHAPTER ONE

"I'm having first go!"

Kenny charged into the bedroom, elbowing the rest of us out of the way. We all squealed loudly, as she sent us flying in all directions.

"No, you're not," Frankie said firmly, sticking her foot out and tripping Kenny up. "It's *my* turn!"

"Ow!" Kenny yelled. She fell forward, and collapsed face-down on the bed. "You little toad, Francesca Thomas!"

"Get her!" Rosie shouted, and we all piled in on top of Kenny, screaming and laughing.

7

Just another normal sleepover, right? Right! You remember all of us, don't you? The Sleepover Club? Well, if you don't, you'll soon work it out!

"I think we should let Fliss have first go," Rosie said in a muffled voice. Frankie was sitting on her head. "After all, she's the only one of us now who hasn't got a computer at home."

Fliss's stepdad Andy did normally have a computer, but it was away being fixed. *Someone* (who shall remain nameless) had spilt nail varnish remover all over the keyboard, and it had gone bonkers!

"Nah, I reckon we should arm-wrestle each other, and the winner gets to go first!" Kenny argued, trying to push me off the bed. I banged into Fliss, and she slid off the duvet and landed on the floor on her backside with a THWACK.

"No, I reckon the *tallest* person should get first go," Frankie said, rolling off Rosie.

"Oh yeah, you would say that, *beanpole*!" Kenny scoffed.

"How about the most *sensible* person?"

Rosie suggested, sitting up and looking smug.

"Oh, you mean *Lyndz*!" Kenny grinned.

"Thanks a lot," I said. "I'm not *that* sensible!"

The reason why we were all fighting over who'd get first go on the computer was because we now had our very own website on the Internet. Yep, the Sleepover Club was online! I don't know if you remember, but we entered a competition to design a Home Page, and we won one of the runners-up prizes, which was to have our Sleepover Club site on the Net. We had a special section where people could send us messages, which was totally *fab*, and we were always arguing over whose turn it was to check them. So far we'd got emails from places like Canada, Norway and Germany – oh, and from Maria and our mates in Spain. (We met them when we went on that school trip, remember?)

"Rosie's right," Frankie agreed. "Let Fliss have first go."

"So long as she hasn't got any nail varnish remover in her bag," I said meaningfully.

Fliss wasn't listening. She was too busy rubbing her bottom, and staring round the room.

"Why do boys' bedrooms always *smell* funny?" she asked, wrinkling up her nose.

My brother Tom's room was a complete tip. There were clothes all over the bed and on the floor, and the desk was covered with paints and books and CDs.

"It's all those horrible smelly socks," Kenny replied. She scooped one off the floor and threw it at Fliss. It hit her smack on the nose.

"Kenny! Don't be so disgusting!" Fliss howled, as everyone else collapsed in giggles.

"Come on, Fliss," I said quickly, before she had a fit. "Frankie's right. *You* have first go."

"Why's the computer in here, anyway, Lyndz?" Rosie asked, as Fliss sat down at the desk. "The Sleepover Club won it, after all."

We'd won the computer in a radio competition in the summer, and the others were letting me look after it. But that's a whole different story!

"Well, Dad's converting the loft into a study," I explained, switching the monitor on, "but there's nowhere else for the computer to go for the moment."

My dad's *always* doing stuff around the house. One minute a wall's there – the next, it isn't! It's like living on a building site.

"It's not fair," Fliss grumbled, flicking her hair off her face. "We're the only ones who haven't got a computer now."

"And whose fault is that?" Kenny snorted.

Fliss ignored her. "I'm going to ask Mum to buy me and Callum one of our own for Christmas."

Kenny winked at us. "I thought your mum asked you if you wanted your own computer *last* Christmas."

Fliss turned pink. "Um – she did," she admitted. "But she said if I got a computer, I couldn't have a whole load of new clothes. So…"

"You went for the clothes," Frankie grinned. "Surprise, surprise!"

Fliss is totally the Queen of Clothes. She's got so many, Kenny says it would take

her ten years to get around to wearing them all.

"So?" Fliss said crossly. "I *need* clothes! I mean, you can't wear a computer, can you?"

"Ooh, I don't know about that." Kenny picked up the keyboard, and balanced it on her head. "And here comes Kenny McKenzie, the first female footballer to play for England, modelling the latest in headgear!"

"Kenny, put it down," I warned her, as the others giggled. "You'll drop it!"

"Stay cool, Lyndz," Kenny said airily, strutting up and down like a supermodel beside the desk. "Look, no hands – oh no!"

Frankie, Rosie and me leapt forward, and grabbed for the keyboard as it fell to the ground. Frankie caught it, one-handed, just before it hit the carpet.

"Nice one, Frankie," Kenny said, looking relieved. "That was a great save – you ought to play for Leicester City! And talking of Leicester City—"

"NO!" the rest of us chorused loudly. Whenever we put any of our computers on,

Kenny always wants to look at mega-boring footie sites.

We had to wait a few seconds for the computer to connect to the Net, then Fliss typed our website address in the box. The Home Page of our site popped up, and we all cheered. We do that *every* time!

"Oh no, I've got to change that stupid photo of me," Frankie groaned, covering her eyes. "I look like I'm about to be sick!"

"You always look like that," Kenny replied, and got an elbow in the ribs.

We've all got our photos on there, underneath *The Sleepover Club* banner. Mine's not too bad, but Kenny's pulling this totally gruesome face – of course! There are sections called *Midnight Feast*, *Sleepover Games* and *Spooky Sleepover Stories*, and loads of information about all the things we get up to when we have sleepovers.

"It's a shame we can't add some more stuff to the site," Kenny grumbled, as Fliss checked the messages section. "We could give people tips on how to set up their own Sleepover Club."

"Yeah, and how to get into loads of trouble at the same time!" Rosie added with a grin.

It's true, we *do* kind of get into trouble every so often, although it's never really our fault. My mum says that wherever the Sleepover Club goes, trouble's never far behind! But what do The Olds know?

"We *can* add stuff to the site if we want to," Frankie said. "My dad's really got into the Net, and he's doing an evening class in web design. So he'll be able to give us a hand."

"Oooh, a message!" Fliss squealed excitedly, bouncing up and down in the chair. "A new message!"

We all crowded round the computer.

"Who sent it?" Kenny asked, "Is it from Chantal in Canada?"

"Is it from Anna in Norway?" Rosie wanted to know.

"Maybe it's from Maria and the others," I suggested.

"Come on, Fliss, get a move on!" Frankie moaned.

"I'm doing my best!" Fliss retorted, fiddling with the mouse. "But it's taking *ages* to open."

"What does that little paperclip thing mean?" Kenny asked, pointing at the screen.

"That means there's something attached to the email," Frankie said. "It could be photos or something."

We were all dead excited. As soon as the email opened up, we all stared at the screen eagerly.

"Hey, it's from the States!" Kenny gasped. "Cool, or what, dude!"

"I can't see," Rosie complained, trying to look over Frankie's shoulder. "Read it out, Fliss."

Hi, Frankie, Fliss, Kenny, Rosie and Lyndz! We are four girls from Miami, who saw your site and think it's just so cool! Our names are Darlene, Barbie, Jennie and Shannon, and we've attached some photos so that you can see what we look like. We love sleepovers, and we're going to start our own club - if our moms and dads let us. They say we get into too much trouble when we're all together, though - just because we accidentally lost Barbie's dog last weekend! (We found him though.)
Please email us back!

"Click on that bit at the bottom of the screen, Fliss," Frankie told her. "Then we can see their photos."

We all waited impatiently for the pictures to load. When they did, the four girls looked really cool. Shannon and Jennie were twins who looked *exactly* the same. Barbie had long black hair and was really pretty, and Darlene was pulling this horrible face that was nearly as bad as Kenny's!

"Shall I write back?" Fliss asked eagerly, her fingers hovering over the keyboard. "What shall I say?"

"Put – Dear Barbie, Jennie, Shannon and Darlene," Rosie began.

"It was totally fab to get your email," I went on.

"We think you should definitely go for it, and start your own Sleepover Club," Frankie added.

"You can get lots of info off our website," Fliss tapped in, "and we can give you loads more. We're the experts!"

"And take no notice of your parents," Kenny instructed, "because *we* don't!"

Fliss typed our names at the bottom, and then hit the Send button. A few seconds later we got a message saying that our email had gone.

"Isn't it totally cool to think that our letter's already on its way to America!" Rosie said. "It's loads quicker than phoning."

"Yeah, I can just see The Olds letting us phone the States," Kenny said, bouncing on to the bed. "They'd have a mega fit!"

"We're lucky we got a chance to use the computer at all," I remarked, as I switched everything off. "Tom's been using it every day since we got it. It's only because he's rehearsing with his band that we got a go today."

"What band?" Frankie asked.

"Oh, Tom's started this band with three of his mates," I replied. "They practise in our garage."

"Your brother Tom's in a pop group?" Fliss's mouth fell open. She looked dead impressed.

I nodded. "Yeah, didn't I mention it?"

"No!" Rosie looked really impressed as well. Honestly, anyone would think it was

Westlife practising in our garage! "What're they called?"

"Aztec," I replied.

"Uh?" Kenny *didn't* look very impressed. "That's well boring. They could have called themselves something really cool – like The Sleepover Club, ha ha!"

"Let's go and check them out," Frankie suggested.

"Yeah, let's get their autographs now, and when they're famous, we can sell them for mega-bucks!" Kenny chortled, jumping off the bed and heading for the door. We all followed, and tried to shove through at the same time.

"Ow!" Fliss yelled. "That was my foot you trod on, Kenny!"

"Last one down loves Ryan Scott!" Kenny shouted, racing for the stairs. Ryan's in our class at school, and Fliss is in love with him anyway, so she didn't mind being last!

We charged into the kitchen, where my mum was making spaghetti and tomato sauce for our tea. Spike, my baby brother, was in his playpen (his name's Sam really,

but his hair sticks up in this cute little spike at the front), and Ben, who's four, was playing with our mad dog, Buster.

"Mum, is it OK if we go into the garage?" I asked. "We want to listen to Tom's band."

My mum smiled. "Are you sure?"

"Why? Are they that bad?" Kenny asked.

"I haven't a clue," my mum replied. "Luckily Lyndz's dad soundproofed the garage, so I don't have to listen to them!"

"They can't be *that* awful," I pointed out. "I mean, they've got their first gig soon."

"A *gig*?" Fliss squealed. She was so excited, I thought she was going to wet herself! "They're actually going to be *playing* somewhere?"

I nodded. "There's a disco at Tom's school in a few weeks' time, and the band are playing there. My dad fixed it up."

My dad's the head of the Art department at the local comp. Tom usually moans like crazy about having to go to the school where Dad teaches, but now he's got a gig for the band out of it, he's shut up!

"Come on then, you lot." I went over to the connecting door, which led from the kitchen

19

into the garage. "Let's sneak in and have a nose around."

I pulled open the door, and immediately a wall of sound hit us.

"*DON'T WANNA GO WITHOUT MY BAY-BEEEE! OH NO!*"

It was mega-loud.

"Shut the door, Lyndz!" my mum yelled, as Ben and Spike both began to bawl. "Now!"

"AWOOOOOOH!" Buster howled, joining in with the singing.

We all hurried into the garage and slammed the door behind us. The music was so loud, Tom and his mates hadn't even noticed us come in. They were all bent over their instruments, shaking their heads in time to the beat.

Frankie nudged me. "Blah blah blah blah?" she said in my ear.

"WHAT?" I yelled back. I couldn't hear a word.

"Blah blah blah BLAH!" Kenny said in my other ear.

"I CAN'T HEAR!" I shouted.

"I DON'T RECKON MUCH TO THIS SONG!" Kenny roared. And we all heard *that* because the song had suddenly finished, and the room was dead quiet. Kenny went as red as a ripe tomato.

"Actually, I don't reckon much to it either, Kenny." Tom grinned at us. "I think we'll drop it, guys. What do you say?"

"Hey, I wrote that song!" said Dan, the drummer, indignantly.

"Tom's right, man," said Liam, who's the lead singer and quite cool (even though I'm not into boys much).

"Nah, I think we should keep it." That was Jack, the other guitarist.

"Oh, great, Kenny," Frankie said. "You've split the band up before they've even done their first gig!"

Kenny shrugged. "Well, that song *was* rubbish!"

"The lead singer's quite cute," Fliss said dreamily.

"Better watch out, Flissy." Kenny elbowed her in the ribs. "Or Ryan Scott will be getting jealous!"

"So, girls, has Lyndz been telling you how it feels to have a superstar for a brother?" Tom came over to us, still carrying his guitar.

"Who's that then?" I asked, raising my eyebrows.

"Funny!" Tom slapped me on the back. "Wait till I'm a famous rock star. I won't give you a ride in my flash car, or on my private jet!"

"Oh, I'm dead upset!" I said, punching him on the shoulder.

Fliss was looking worried. "What if his band *does* become famous, Lyndz?" she whispered anxiously. "You'd better be nice to him."

The others started giggling, but Fliss really *was* serious!

"Yeah, Fliss is right, Lyndz," Tom said with a grin. "You can start by buying me a really cool present for my birthday – a sports car would be great!"

"What's up, Lyndz?" Frankie asked, as Tom went back to join the rest of the band. "You've suddenly got a face on you like a totally wet weekend."

"I forgot Tom's birthday was coming up," I said, biting my lip. "And I've just gone and spent all my money on new riding gear. I haven't got enough left to buy him a prezzie."

"I don't think he *really* wants a sports car!" Rosie said.

"I can't even afford to buy him a card with a *picture* of a sports car," I sighed. I couldn't believe I'd been so daft. I'd been saving for ages, and I really needed new jodhpurs and a riding hat. But if I'd remembered Tom's birthday was coming up, I could've waited a bit longer. "I could kick myself."

"I'll do it for you, if you like," Kenny joked, trying to cheer me up.

"Hey, brilliant idea alert!" Frankie whispered suddenly.

"I'm not borrowing any money from you lot," I said firmly. "It'll take me ages to pay it back."

"It's not that." Frankie beckoned to us, and we all went into a huddle, like an American football team. "We could design a website for Tom about his band, and put it on the Net as a birthday surprise. What about it, guys?"

CHAPTER TWO

"We could do, like, a questionnaire thing for each member of the band," Kenny suggested eagerly. "You know: what's your favourite food, what's your favourite colour, that kind of stuff."

"That's a great idea, Kenny," I said, scribbling it down on my notepad. We'd all rushed off to my bedroom to plan the website, and we were looking at some of my old copies of *Popstar* magazine, to get some ideas.

"How are we going to ask things like that without them getting suspicious?" Rosie wanted to know.

"We'll just have to be really clever about it," I replied. "Anyway, Liam, Jack and Dan have been Tom's mates for years – I already know quite a bit about them."

"We ought to find out their star signs too." Fliss pointed to a page in *Popstar* magazine, headed *Star Horoscopes*.

I wrote that down as well. "This is such a cool idea, Frankie," I said gratefully. "Tom's going to be well pleased."

"And best of all, it won't cost any cash!" Kenny said with a grin. "Hey, shouldn't we have some photos of the band on there too?"

"Yeah, good idea," Frankie agreed. "Have you got that camera your dad bought, Lyndz?"

I nodded.

"What about a film?" Fliss asked.

Frankie grinned. "It doesn't need one," she said.

Fliss, Kenny and Rosie stared at her.

"Don't be daft, Francesca," Kenny said. "You can't take pictures without a film!"

"You can if it's a *digital* camera," Frankie explained. "My dad's got one. The camera takes the picture, and then you connect the

camera to your computer, and you can see the photo on the computer screen. Simple."

We were all dead impressed.

"You know, Frankie, you're in serious danger of turning into a computer nerd!" Kenny said, giving her a shove.

"What, instead of a football nerd like you, you mean?" Frankie retorted, swiping her round the head with a rolled-up copy of *Popstar*.

"OK, what else?" I asked, looking at my list. But before anyone could say anything, my mum yelled up the stairs that tea was ready.

"Liam, Jack and Dan usually stay for tea when they come round to practise," I told the others, as we clattered down the stairs. "So we can find out loads of stuff for the website."

"And remember, we don't want them to guess what's going on," Kenny instructed us. "So play it dead cool. Right— *Aaargh!*"

Kenny had jumped down the last few stairs into the hall, and landed on the rug, which skidded on the polished wooden floor.

Kenny skidded along with it, and ended up in a tangled heap in the kitchen doorway. The rest of us nearly died laughing.

"Great entrance, Kenny!" Tom called. He and his mates were already sitting at the kitchen table, scoffing Mum's spaghetti.

"Yeah, that was dead cool, Kenny!" Frankie whispered, hauling her to her feet.

We all crammed in round the kitchen table. It was lucky my oldest brother Stuart was out with his girlfriend, and Dad was still at work, or we'd never have fitted. I noticed that Fliss nearly knocked Frankie and Rosie over so that she could grab the seat next to Liam – she really had it bad!

"I like your shirt, Liam," Fliss said brightly, as Mum started heaping spaghetti on to our plates. "Is blue your favourite colour?"

Liam looked a bit surprised.

"Well, yeah, I guess so," he said.

Fliss immediately started pulling faces at me, and raising her eyebrows.

"OK, OK," I muttered, quickly writing *Liam – blue* on my notepad. I'd brought it down with me, and had it hidden on my lap.

"What're you doing, Lyndz?" Mum asked. Why do parents always seem to have eyes in the backs of their heads?

"Nothing," I said, hiding the notepad under a corner of the tablecloth.

Kenny turned to Tom. "What's *your* favourite colour then?" she asked.

"Er – purple," Tom replied, looking as if he thought Kenny had gone totally mad. OK, maybe they all thought we were a bit strange, but we carried on until we'd found out *all* their favourite colours!

Then Rosie started off again. "Mm, I love spaghetti," she said. "It's my favourite food!" She stared hard at Jack. "What's *your* favourite food?"

By the time we'd scoffed Mum's toffee apple pudding, we'd found out *loads* of stuff! I think Tom and the others couldn't wait to get away from us and our endless questions though, because they legged it back into the garage as soon as they'd finished their pud.

"What are you girls up to?" Mum asked suspiciously, as she cleared the dishes away.

"Nothing," we all chorused.

"That always means *something*." Mum raised her eyebrows at us. But luckily Spike threw his plastic bowl of yucky yellow baby food at Buster just then, so we were able to make our escape.

We decided that next we'd take some photos, so I got the digital camera, and Frankie showed us how to work it. It was totally brilliant. You took a picture, and then the camera showed you how it looked, so you could decide if you liked it, or if you wanted to take another one before you put it on the computer.

"OK, leave all the talking to me," Kenny told the rest of us, as we dashed downstairs again with the camera.

"Yeah, don't forget to play it cool!" Frankie teased, as Kenny stepped carefully over the hall rug.

"Won't the band think it's a bit weird that we want to take their photos?" Rosie asked.

"I told you, leave all the talking to me," Kenny said breezily. "We can say that Fliss is in love with Liam, and she's dying for a photo of him."

29

"Don't you dare, Kenny!" Fliss squealed.

Tom and the band didn't look that thrilled to see us, when we all piled into the garage again. I guess we were starting to get on their nerves a bit.

"Don't mind us," Kenny called, beginning to snap away with the camera as if she was some sort of newspaper photographer. "We just want to get a few pictures, that's all."

"Why?" asked Liam.

Fliss turned pink, and hid behind Rosie, in case Kenny dropped her in it.

"Oh, no reason," Kenny said, still snapping away.

Frankie rolled her eyes. "I thought you said leave all the talking to you!" she hissed, as the boys looked even more confused.

"Look, they'll let us take as many photos as we want, if they think it'll get rid of us!" Kenny whispered. "Go on, Tom, stand next to Liam, will you?"

Kenny managed to get quite a few pics before the boys got fed up. When Tom started giving me the evil eye, I decided that it was time we left them to it. Giggling madly,

we raced upstairs and had a look through the pics Kenny had taken. We decided which ones we were going to use, and then we deleted the rest.

"Come on, let's design the website," Frankie said eagerly. So we got some big pieces of paper, lay on my bedroom floor and began to work out where everything was going to go. To start with, we decided to have *Aztec* in great big letters at the top of the Home Page, with a photo of the band underneath. Then Kenny suggested that we did a kind of guide to each member of the band, with a photo and loads of info about them. So we started trying to sort that out. It took *ages*, and we weren't even half-finished before my mum came in and told us it was time for bed.

"Thanks, guys," I said gratefully, rolling up the bits of paper we'd been working on. "This website is going to be so *cool*. Tom's going to love it."

"Last one into the bathroom's a hairy chimp!" Kenny yelled, grabbing her pyjamas and toothbrush from her sleepover bag.

We all scrambled for our stuff, and dashed along the landing. Just as we rushed past Tom's bedroom, the door opened and my brother came out.

"Oh, so it *wasn't* a herd of elephants after all!" he said teasingly. "Sure you don't want to ask me any more questions, like what my favourite animal is, or something?"

"No," I said, thinking I'd better change the subject – fast. "What're you up to?"

"I've just finished designing the publicity poster on the computer for our first gig," Tom replied. "Want to take a look?"

"Sure," I replied.

We all crowded into Tom's room, and looked at the computer screen. The poster was fab. It had the word *Aztec* in the middle, which was written in curly letters in different shades of purple, and then there was a kind of sunburst of purples, greens and gold around the lettering.

"Wow!" Frankie said admiringly. "That must've been really difficult. I bet my dad couldn't do that!"

"Well, my technology teacher at school

helped," Tom said, fiddling with the keyboard. "I'm just copying it on to disk, then I'm going to take it into school and photocopy it."

He clicked the disk out of the machine, and then wrote on the label:

```
INDEX
Very important!

Property of Tom Collins
```

"You know what?" Kenny said in a low voice as we went out. "That poster would look fab on our website!"

"Ooh, yeah!" Fliss said eagerly, and everyone else nodded.

"If we got hold of that disk, we could copy the poster on to a blank one," Frankie whispered. "Tom would never know."

We all glanced over our shoulders, and saw Tom slip the disk into the side pocket of his school bag.

"Let's wait till he's gone downstairs,"

Kenny suggested, elbowing her way into the bathroom ahead of the rest of us. "Hey, Fliss, you're last – you're the hairy chimp!"

"Oh, very funny," Fliss sniffed. "And don't try putting a blob of toothpaste down my neck like you did at our last sleepover!"

"OK," Kenny agreed. She squeezed a big lump of toothpaste on to her brush, and dropped it down the back of Rosie's T-shirt instead.

"*Kenny*!" Rosie howled, jumping up and down.

We finally managed to get into our pyjamas and get our teeth cleaned. On our way back across the landing, we noticed that Tom's bedroom door was open. He wasn't there, and the computer was still on…

"Come on," Kenny whispered. "This is our chance!"

We all tiptoed into Tom's bedroom.

"We need a blank disk to copy the poster on to," Frankie said, hunting around on the desk.

"Hurry up!" Fliss was nearly wetting herself. "I can hear someone coming!"

Sure enough, there were footsteps coming

up the stairs. We all panicked, and leapt for the door. We rushed into my room, just as Tom appeared on the landing.

"That was close!" Rosie breathed.

"Do you think we'll get a chance to copy it later?" Fliss asked.

"Sure we will!" Kenny beamed. She slipped her hand into the pocket of her pyjamas, and pulled out a computer disk. It was labelled:

```
INDEX
Very important!
Property of Tom Collins
```

"I nicked it out of his bag while the rest of you were panicking," Kenny explained. "Now we can take it over to Frankie's tomorrow morning and copy it. Simple!"

Well, it *sounded* simple, didn't it? But guess what?

It wasn't!

CHAPTER THREE

"Yeah, Lyndz, I've still got the disk." Kenny waved it at me, then put it back in her coat pocket. "That must be the ten millionth time you've asked me!"

"Sorry," I said. "It's just that Tom's put so much work into it. He'll kill me if we lose it!"

It was the following morning. After breakfast we'd decided to go on to Frankie's house, so that we could copy the poster and get on with designing the website. We were going to ask Mr Thomas if he'd give us a hand, too. We'd just stopped off at Rosie's and Fliss's houses so they could drop their

sleepover bags off, and now we were on our way to Kenny's.

"I hope Tom doesn't notice the disk is missing," I said worriedly.

"Look, it'll be back in his bag by this afternoon, Lyndz," Frankie said. "He doesn't need it till he goes to school on Monday, anyway."

"Yeah, Frankie's right." Kenny rang the McKenzies' doorbell. "Nothing's gonna go wrong, Lyndz. Don't worry so much!"

Yeah, right...

Molly the Monster, Kenny's older sister, opened the door, and looked down her nose at us. "What do you lot want?" she said rudely.

"I live here, remember?" Kenny pushed past her, and we all followed. Kenny and Molly really hate each other, and they have to share a bedroom which drives Kenny bananas.

"Don't think you're going to hang out in our room!" Molly snapped, chasing us up the stairs, "'Cos me and Louise are in there, listening to CDs."

"Who's Louise?" Frankie asked.

"Louise Ball, she's a mate of Molly's," Kenny explained. "Yeah, strange as it may seem, she has actually got *one* friend!"

"I heard that, Laura McKenzie!" Molly howled furiously.

We all piled into Kenny's bedroom. A weedy-looking girl was sitting on Molly's bed, glaring at us.

"What do you think, guys?" Kenny winked at us. "Shall we hang around here, and annoy Molly the Monster and Louise the Leech?"

Molly went purple. "Just get lost, Kenny!" she snapped.

"And take your snotty-nosed little mates with you," Louise added snootily.

"*What* did you call my friends?" Kenny asked, taking a step towards Louise. She actually looked quite frightened. Well, Kenny *can* be a bit scary when she gets going.

"Come on, Kenny," Frankie said firmly, taking her arm and hustling her out of the room. "Let's go to my place and get on with you-know-what."

"Yeah, the sooner we get that disk copied,

the better," I chimed in, as we went downstairs. "I *have* to replace it before Tom notices it's gone."

"Who does Molly the Monster think she is?" Kenny grumbled, as we went on to Frankie's house. "It's about time I played another trick on her. I haven't done anything since I put custard in her trainers!"

"Hi, girls." Frankie's dad was out on the drive, washing the car. He waved as we walked towards him. "How's things? No disasters last night at the Collins' house then?"

"Oh, *Dad*," Frankie groaned. "You make it sound like *every* sleepover's a disaster."

Mr Thomas raised his eyebrows. "I'm not saying another word!"

"If you're not nice to us, we won't let you help us with our new website," Frankie said with a grin.

Mr Thomas looked interested. "What website is that? And, Kenny, put that sponge down!"

Kenny was sneaking up behind Fliss and Rosie, holding the sopping wet sponge.

Pulling a face, she chucked it back into the bucket, while me and Frankie explained about Tom and his band and the website.

Mr Thomas was dead pleased to be asked to help, because it meant he'd get the chance to show off all the stuff he'd learnt about web design at his evening class. He promised that as soon as we'd finished designing the site, he'd put it all together, and it'd be ready for Tom's birthday. Cool or what?

"Everything's working out brilliantly!" Frankie said, as we raced up the stairs to her bedroom. Mrs Thomas had taken Frankie's baby sister, Izzy, out for a walk, so we had the place to ourselves. "If we can finish designing the website this weekend, then Dad'll have plenty of time to start setting it up."

"We'd better copy the poster first," Kenny suggested.

"Nah, let's check the Sleepover Club site, and see if those American girls have replied," Fliss said, as Frankie switched the computer on.

"Whose turn is it?" Rosie asked.

We all groaned.

"Mine." Frankie plonked herself firmly down in front of the computer, and logged on to the Internet. "I gave Fliss my go this morning."

We all waited impatiently for our site to pop up on the screen. When Frankie checked the messages section, we were well pleased to see that we had *two* new emails!

"Look, one's from those American girls, and one's from someone called Katie Shaw." Frankie frowned. "We've never had any messages from a Katie Shaw before, have we?"

"No," I agreed, "and look, the title's *Very Important!*. Maybe we should read that one first."

"Nah, let's read the American one first." Kenny pointed at the screen. "Look, it's called *Our First Sleepover Disaster*!"

Frankie opened up the email, and we all gathered round to read it.

Dear Frankie, Fliss, Kenny, Lyndz and Rosie,
We're emailing you in the middle of our sleepover! It's late at night here, and we're staying at Shannon's place. We just snuck downstairs to raid the fridge, and guess

what? On the way back, we accidentally broke Shannon's mum's favourite ornament! It's this funny–looking clown with a big hat on, and Darlene knocked it over and broke the hat off!

What do you think we should do? Should we confess in the morning, or should we hide the bits, and pretend we don't know anything about it?

Please email us back!

We couldn't help laughing.

"Hey, that's just what happened to us ages ago!" Kenny pointed out. "When we were trying to make that video to send to *You've Been Framed*, remember?"

"You mean when you put those ice-cubes down my pyjamas, Kenny," Fliss said with a wince.

"And you jumped and whacked me with that plate of biscuits you were holding, Fliss," Rosie added.

"And I leapt out of the way, and I knocked that ornament over and broke it," Frankie remembered.

"And we didn't want Fliss's mum to find out, so we glued it back together," I finished off.

"That's what we'll tell them then." Kenny grinned. "Tell them to glue it back together, and no-one'll know the difference!"

Frankie began typing furiously. Then she clicked the Send button, and the email whizzed off, or whatever it does.

"Darlene and her mates sound as if they're always getting into trouble," I remarked.

Kenny pointed out, "Well, at least we can help them to get themselves *out* of it!"

"We got found out when we broke Mrs Proudlove's ornament though," Rosie reminded us.

"That was only because Fliss left the camcorder with the tape in it lying around," Kenny retorted.

"If Kenny hadn't put the ice-cubes down my neck, Frankie wouldn't have broken the ornament in the first place!" Fliss snapped.

"Guys, guys, *guys*!" Frankie yelled. She was staring at the computer screen as if her eyes were glued to it. "I've just opened that email from Katie Shaw. I think you'd better all read it. And fast."

We all crowded round the screen again.

To whom it may concern,
I have a computer disk which belongs to Tom Collins, and
I think you might just want it back as soon as possible.
It will cost you a ransom of five pounds.

Katie Shaw

CHAPTER FOUR

Our eyes nearly fell out of our heads. We just couldn't *believe* what we were reading.

"It's a wind-up, right?" I stammered. "I mean, how could this Katie Shaw, whoever she is, have Tom's disk?"

"She can't," Rosie said. "We all *know* where the disk is."

"Safely tucked away in Kenny's pocket," Frankie chimed in.

"Go on, Kenny," Fliss urged. "Get the disk and show us!"

Kenny almost fell over her feet in her eagerness to grab her coat, which she'd

45

slung on to Frankie's bed. Looking confident, she put her hand in her pocket. Then her face dropped. She put her hand in the other pocket, and her face dropped even further.

"Kenny!" I gasped, feeling my heart sink right down to my toes. "Where *is* it?"

"I dunno." Looking increasingly frantic, Kenny searched through the pockets of her sweatpants. "I'm sure I had it when we left my house. Well, pretty sure…"

I was so upset, I felt like crying. "Where *can* it be?" I muttered.

Fliss put her arm round me. "Don't worry, Lyndz, we'll find it somehow," she said comfortingly.

"Yeah, sorry, Lyndz," Kenny mumbled. She looked almost as upset as I was.

"So do you think this Katie Shaw really *has* got the disk then?" Frankie asked. She was still staring at the email. "She knows it's Tom's. Maybe she's read the label on it."

We all looked at each other.

"I suppose she *might* have," Rosie said at last.

"Or she might be trying to get five quid out of us for nothing," Kenny said, glaring at the screen. "This is blackmail!"

"But how does Katie Shaw, whoever she is, know that we've lost the disk, if she hasn't got it?" Frankie asked.

"Yeah, she *must* have it," I agreed.

"Maybe we should ask for some proof," Fliss suggested.

"That's a brilliant idea, Flissy." Kenny slapped her on the back. "Quick, Frankie, write back and say we don't believe she's got the disk. She's got to prove it to us."

Frankie quickly typed an answer.

We don't believe you've got the disk. You'll have to give us some proof.

Then she hit the Send button.

"OK, well, we're just going to have to wait for Katie Shaw to reply," Kenny said grimly, folding her arms. I didn't fancy Katie's chances much if she *had* got the disk – Kenny looked like she was ready to eat someone for breakfast!

"I can't sit around waiting for a reply," I wailed. "I'll have no fingernails left!"

"Maybe we should go and look for the disk," Rosie suggested. "We could walk back the same route we came this morning."

"Yeah, good idea," Frankie agreed, switching the computer off.

I don't really think any of us thought we'd find the disk, but it was better than sitting around doing nothing. So we all dashed down the stairs again, and out of the house. Frankie's dad was just hosing down the car. He looked really surprised to see us.

"Just going down the shop, Dad," Frankie said quickly, "We're out of – er – Coca-Cola."

"Oh really." Frankie's dad eyeballed us suspiciously. "What happened to those three big bottles we bought at the supermarket this morning?"

"Is it the brown sort?" Kenny wanted to know.

Frankie's dad blinked. "Of course it is. What other sort is there?"

"I can't drink that," Kenny said innocently.

"I'm allergic to it. I have to have that new Coca-Cola. It's – er – green."

"*Green*?" Mr Thomas's eyebrows nearly shot off the top of his head.

"Won't be long, Dad," Frankie called, as we raced off down the road.

"Green Coca-Cola?" Fliss giggled. "Couldn't you think of a better excuse than that, Kenny?"

"Well, I didn't see the rest of you helping Frankie out!" Kenny grumbled. "It was the best I could think of."

"Never mind that," I said urgently. "Just keep your eyes peeled and see if you can spot that disk!"

We walked slowly back to Kenny's house the way we'd come that morning. The last time Kenny had shown me the disk was just after we'd left the Proudloves, so we went all the way back to Fliss's. But we didn't find anything. The disk had well and truly vanished.

"We'd better go back to Frankie's and see if Katie Shaw's replied yet," Fliss said at last.

"Hey, wait a minute!" Frankie yelled,

stopping dead in the middle of the pavement. "Francesca Thomas saves the day yet again!"

We all stared.

"Look, Tom doesn't *need* the disk," Frankie gabbled excitedly. "He's got the poster stored on his hard drive!"

Fliss looked blank. "His what?"

"The computer's memory," Frankie explained. "The disk Tom made was only a copy, so he can just take *another* copy off the hard drive. Simple!"

"Great!" Kenny looked mightily relieved, and everyone started cheering and doing high fives. Except me.

"Sorry, Frankie," I sighed. "Tom said a few days ago that as soon as he'd made a copy, he was going to *delete* it because the poster took up too much space on the hard drive. He probably did it last night."

Everyone's faces dropped again. Gloomily we trudged back to Frankie's in silence. I didn't know what I was going to do. I had to get that disk back – but I didn't have five pounds to pay Katie Shaw. I didn't even have

five *pence*. I just hoped she didn't really have it. But if she didn't, then where could it be?

Mr Thomas was vacuuming the inside of the car when we got back. He looked at us suspiciously.

"Where is it then?" he asked.

"What?" we chorused.

Mr Thomas stared hard at us. "The green Coca-Cola."

"I drank it," Kenny chirped up. Then she did this totally realistic burp. "Oh, excuse me!"

Frankie's dad watched us hurry into the house. "I hope you girls aren't up to something us parents aren't going to like," he called after us.

"Honestly, Dad!" Frankie called back, "Would we do such a thing?"

"Yes," said Mr Thomas.

Frankie shut the door quickly behind us, and we all ran upstairs. "Why do our parents never *trust* us?" she grumbled, switching the computer on. "It really gets on my nerves!"

"Quick, Frankie, hurry up and see if there's a message," I urged her. "*Hic!* Oh no, I've – *hic* – got hiccups!"

"You've been drinking too much green Coca-Cola!" Kenny grinned, slapping me on the back.

"Hic!" I tried to hold my breath. The others call me the Hiccup Queen, 'cos I get them so often. "Are there any – *hic* – new messages, Frankie?"

"Yeah, there's one from Katie Shaw!" Frankie replied, clicking quickly on the mouse.

The email popped open, and we all gathered round to read it.

I've looked at the disk, and it's got a poster on it for a band called Aztec. The poster's decorated in purples, greens and golds, with all this fancy writing. NOW do you believe I've got it??????

We stared at each other in silence.

"She HAS got it!" I gasped. At least the shock had cured my hiccups! "What are we going to do now?"

"I'll show you!" Kenny replied furiously. "Move over, Frankie."

Kenny plonked herself down in front of the computer and began to type furiously.

OK, game over, Katie Shaw, whoever you are. That disk isn't yours, so you're handling stolen goods! You'd better give it back right away or your life won't be worth living...
The Sleepover Club

"Kenny, maybe that's not the best thing to say—" Fliss began, but it was too late. Kenny had already hit the button, and sent it.

"That'll show *her*!" Kenny said with satisfaction. "You wait, we'll get a grovelling email, offering to give us the disk back straight away."

"Look!" Rosie pointed at the screen. "She's replied already!"

Sure enough, a new email from Katie Shaw had popped straight into our inbox. Kenny could hardly click the mouse fast enough to open it up.

The price has now gone up to six pounds. And it's going up by a pound a day, every day.

"WHAT!" Kenny shrieked, bouncing up and down angrily in her chair. "I don't believe it!"

"She's got a nerve!" Frankie exclaimed furiously.

"As well as our disk!" Rosie added gloomily.

"What are we going to *do*?" I asked. "We don't even know who she is."

Fliss cleared her throat. "Maybe we do," she said.

We were all moaning so much, it took a few seconds for what Fliss had said to sink in. Then we all pounced on her.

"Fliss! Do you know who it is?" Kenny demanded.

"I'm not *certain* sure," Fliss said slowly. "But I've got an idea…"

"Who?" Frankie and Rosie asked together.

"Well, I'm not really sure—" Fliss began again.

"FLISS!" we all yelled, "Just tell us!"

"OK, there's no need to shout." Fliss looked offended. "I just wondered if it could be Catherine Shaw, you know, that girl at school."

"Catherine Shaw!" we all chorused together. We knew exactly who Fliss meant.

"How would she know our email address?" I asked.

"Everyone at school knows about our website, remember?" Fliss reminded me. "We did that assembly about it at school when we won the competition. It'd be easy for Catherine to look it up."

"But do people call her Katie?" Rosie asked.

"No, most people call her 'that big bully'!" Kenny replied. "You know what she's like…"

We all looked nervous. Catherine Shaw wasn't just a bit of a bully, she was a pain in the neck as well. If she had our disk, even Kenny'd think twice about going after *her*…

CHAPTER FIVE

"There she is." Kenny nudged me, and nodded across the playground.

It was Monday morning, just before the bell rang, and we were trailing Catherine Shaw like detectives in a cop show. We'd already followed her to the shop on the corner, and seen her scoff two Twixes and a bag of Doritos. Now she was wandering round the playground, nicking sweets off some of the younger kids.

"I'd forgotten how big she is," Fliss muttered. She was actually shivering! "I hope it isn't her who's got it."

56

"Well, it was your idea, Flissy, and it's the best one we've got so far," Kenny retorted. "Now we've got to decide what we're going to do."

"Well, we could ask her straight out if she's got the disk," Rosie suggested.

"Any volunteers?" Frankie looked round at the rest of us. All our hands stayed firmly down, even Kenny's.

"Maybe we could try and get a look in her bag," Kenny said, staring longingly at Catherine's black rucksack.

"Come on," Frankie hissed, "she's on the move again!"

We all crept round the side of the school, keeping our eyes glued to Catherine. She hadn't noticed us following her, so far…

"What do you lot think you're doing?" asked a gruff voice behind us. We all nearly jumped out of our skins. Guess who it was? The Terrible Twins, of course. Emily Berryman and Emma Hughes – our total worst enemies.

"Take a hike, Berryman," Kenny growled, deliberately copying Emily's gruff voice. "This is none of your business!"

"You're up to something," the Goblin went on suspiciously. "They're up to something, aren't they, Emma?"

Emma Hughes, or the Queen as we call her, looked down her snooty nose at us.

"Definitely," she agreed. "Why are you spying on Catherine Shaw?"

"We're not," said Frankie, Fliss, Kenny and I together, at *exactly* the same moment Rosie said, "So what if we are?" Which kind of gave the game away, a bit.

"You ARE spying on Catherine Shaw!" the Queen said triumphantly. "Maybe we should go and tell her, Emma."

We glanced at each other in dismay. The M&Ms could ruin *everything*.

"Go on then," Kenny said breezily. "And if she doesn't believe you, she'll probably smack you one in the chops!"

Emma and Emily's faces both fell. They knew as well as we did that Catherine Shaw was the kind of person who thumped first and asked questions later. And the Queen and the Goblin are both mega-weedy types – even Fliss isn't scared of *them*!

"Come on, Emily." The Queen linked arms with the Goblin, and they both stuck their noses in the air. "We'll find out what they're up to – and then we'll drop them right in it with Catherine Shaw!"

We glared at the M&Ms as they sauntered off.

"You don't think *they* could have the disk, do you?" Frankie asked in a low voice. "It's just the sort of trick they'd love to pull over us."

Kenny frowned. "Nah, I don't think so. They would've been all smug and *I-know-something-you-don't-know*."

"Anyway, how could the Queen and the Goblin be sending us emails from a Katie Shaw?" Rosie wanted to know.

"They could be using someone else's email address," Frankie suggested.

That gobsmacked us a bit. We hadn't thought of that.

"Maybe we'd better keep an eye on *them*, as well as Catherine Shaw," I said. "OUCH!"

Ryan Scott had just come dashing round the corner, and banged right into me, sending me flying.

"Ryan, you complete idiot!" Frankie said crossly, pulling me to my feet. "Why don't you look where you're going?"

"EEK!" Fliss shrieked, as Ryan's dozy mate, Danny McCloud, came racing after him and bumped right into *her*.

We all glared at them.

"What're you girls doing lurking around here anyway?" Ryan demanded. "You're up to something! They're up to something, aren't they, Danny?"

"Yeah." Danny nodded. "We saw you following Catherine Shaw to the sweet shop."

"Oh, shove off and leave us alone," Kenny snapped.

"Fliss'll tell us, won't you, Fliss?" Ryan grinned at her, and Fliss turned pink.

"Um – er – well," she stuttered, before Kenny clapped a hand over her mouth.

"Push off, Ryan," Frankie ordered him. "And take your dopey friend with you."

"Who's that?" Danny asked dozily.

We all started giggling, as Ryan and Danny went off.

"Hey, you don't think it could be Ryan and Danny sending us those emails, do you?" Rosie asked. "You know how they like playing tricks on people."

"Yeah, you could be right," Frankie agreed. "Like I said before, whoever it is could be using someone else's email address."

"Maybe we'd better keep an eye on Ryan and Danny as well as the M&Ms, *and* Catherine Shaw," I suggested.

"Talking of Catherine Shaw…" Kenny nodded across the playground. "Look!"

Catherine had decided to muscle in on a gang of boys playing football. She was bossing them around, and pushing them over every time they tried to tackle her and get the ball. The boys were too weedy to stop her, so they just let her go on and score a goal.

"She's chucked her rucksack down on that bench," Kenny said. She had this glint in her eye which always meant she was about to do something completely barmy.

"Kenny!" Fliss squeaked. "You're not going to look in Catherine's bag, are you?"

"She might not be carrying the disk around with her," Rosie pointed out.

"Well, it's worth a try, isn't it?"

Kenny started to sidle across the playground, keeping an eye on Catherine as she did so. The rest of us followed, even though Fliss could hardly walk because her knees were knocking together so much.

"Cover me!" Kenny whispered out of the side of her mouth, as if she was a New York cop or something. So the rest of us gathered round the bench, and tried to look casual. We did our best to hide Kenny, as she started rooting in the side pockets of Catherine's rucksack.

"Oi! What are you lot doing!"

We all nearly *died* as Catherine Shaw came charging across the playground towards us. She had this look on her face that scared *me* to death, never mind Fliss!

"What are you doing with my rucksack?" Catherine demanded, folding her arms and advancing menacingly towards us.

"Nothing," Kenny said quickly. I think she was the only one of us who could still speak.

"I feel sick," Fliss moaned.

Catherine shot an uneasy glance at Fliss, then eyeballed Kenny.

"What were you doing with my rucksack, McKenzie?"

"I was just moving it aside so that Fliss could sit down," Kenny replied. "She's not feeling well."

"I think I'm going to be sick!" Fliss groaned. "Quick, give me that!" And she grabbed Catherine's rucksack, and bent her head over it.

"Don't you dare!" Catherine howled furiously. She pulled the rucksack away from Fliss and stormed off, shooting us a poisonous glare as she did so.

"Well done, Fliss." Frankie slapped her on the back. "That was brilliant."

Fliss smiled weakly. "I really *did* feel sick when I thought Catherine Shaw was going to have a go at us!"

"Did you see the disk when you had your head over the bag?" asked Kenny hopefully.

Fliss shook her head. "Sorry."

"So we're still no nearer to finding out if

she's got the disk," Rosie said. "What are we going to do *now*?"

It was a good question, but nobody seemed to have any answers.

"Tom'll have found out that the disk is missing by now," I said worriedly, as we walked home at the end of the day. Everyone was coming round to my place to check if Katie Shaw had sent us any more emails, and to do some more work on the Aztec website (although none of us felt like it, much). "I bet he's going crazy looking for it. I feel—"

"Really sorry for him, yeah, we know," sighed Kenny. "Don't worry, Lyndz. We'll get that disk back. We'll get it back if it's the last thing we do."

"It probably will be, if Catherine Shaw's got it!" Frankie joked. She was trying to cheer everyone up, but nobody laughed. We just didn't have a clue what we were going to do next.

When we got to my place, my mum was in the living room with Ben and Spike, who

were watching *The Lion King*. Mum was looking pretty stressed out.

"Lyndz, Tom's going mad looking for a computer disk he's lost," she said. "You haven't seen it, have you?"

I swallowed. "Not recently," I said. Which was true enough.

"Oh, blast." My mum sighed. "You were our last hope. Tom said you girls were using the computer when you were here for the sleepover, so we thought you might have seen it."

"We saw Tom put it in his schoolbag," Kenny chimed in. Which was also true enough.

"Where's Tom now?" I asked.

"Searching his room – for the millionth time!" my mum replied. "It's such a shame. He put so much work into designing that poster for the gig."

We all crept out of the living room and up the stairs, feeling completely shamefaced. As we reached the landing we could hear bangs and thumps, and other loud noises. Tom's bedroom door was open, and he was pulling all the books off his bookshelves and flinging

them on the floor. He was red in the face, and looked totally cheesed off.

"Hey, Lyndz," he called hopefully, "have you seen that disk? You know, the one with my poster on it?"

"We saw you put it in your bag," I said carefully, and the others nodded.

"I know." Tom shook his head, looking completely bewildered. "But when I got to school this morning, it wasn't there. I just can't believe it!"

I felt *really* lousy. So did the others, from the looks on their faces. We all stood there, shuffling our feet and clearing our throats. We must have looked dead guilty, but Tom didn't seem to notice.

"The posters should really have gone up this week," he muttered, flicking through the papers on his desk. "If I don't find the disk in the next couple of days, I'm going to have to design a new one."

Wow! Relief or what! We all looked at each other, and Frankie gave us a thumbs-up.

"But I won't have enough time to do a really cool design like I did before," Tom

went on miserably. "It'll just have to be something simple."

So then we were really depressed again.

"Tom?" That was my mum calling from downstairs. "The rest of the band is here."

"OK," Tom called back. Then he turned to me. "Gotta go, I've got a rehearsal," he said. "But if you find the disk, come and tell me straight away, all right?"

"All right," I agreed. Fat chance.

"This is awful," Frankie muttered, as Tom went out.

"I feel really mean," Fliss said.

"Me too," Rosie agreed.

Kenny didn't say anything. I guess she felt the worst because she was the one who'd lost the disk, but I'd never seen her so quiet.

We put the computer on, and checked our site. We had two new emails. One was from Katie Shaw, and it said simply:

The ransom money is now seven pounds. Pay up or you don't get your disk back!

"I'm getting well sick of this Katie Shaw!" Rosie said crossly, hitting the Delete button.

"Maybe we should think about paying the ransom after all," I said hesitantly. "I could sell my new riding hat. Someone at the stables would probably buy it off me."

But the others were shaking their heads.

"We can't give in, just like that!" Frankie said firmly.

"We've still got a bit of time left to try and get the disk back ourselves," Rosie added.

"And anyway, even if we pay the money, we might not get the disk back," Fliss pointed out. "That's what blackmailers do in the films – they take the money, and then try and get *more* out of you!"

Fliss was right. I hadn't thought of that. I looked at Kenny, as she was the only one who hadn't said anything – but she didn't even look like she was listening.

The second email was from Darlene and the others. They'd managed to repair the broken ornament, and apart from getting glue all over the carpet which they'd had to scrape up, they were fine. And Shannon's

mum hadn't even noticed that the clown's hat had been knocked off and replaced!

"Let's tell them what's been happening to us," Fliss suggested, so we typed in this long message, telling them all about Tom's band and the disk and the blackmailer. Then we sent it off.

"I forgot to tell you," Frankie said, as we went to my bedroom, "my dad's started doing the Aztec website. It's looking really good so far."

"We'd better get on with the rest of it then," I said. I didn't feel like doing any more on the website at all – it just kept reminding me of how important that lost computer disk was. But now that Mr Thomas was working so hard on it, it would be a bit mean to stop. And, anyway, I still needed a birthday present for Tom.

We spread all our notes out over my bedroom floor, and got to work. We finished sorting out the info about the different band members, and Frankie had this really brilliant idea of writing the words in their favourite colours, so that all the stuff about

Liam was written in blue ink and Tom's was written in purple. Meanwhile, Rosie and Fliss were doing a horoscopes page (we'd managed to find out the boys' birthdays), and we had a list of all the songs the band had written, which we were going to put on the site too.

After a bit, we started really getting into the website again, which was great, because it took our minds off everything that had happened over the last few days. But Kenny was still really quiet. And that usually means trouble...

"Kenny, pass me that purple felt-tip, will you?" I asked.

"RIGHT!" Kenny said, all of a sudden. "I've had ENOUGH!"

I stared at her. "Don't get your knickers in a twist," I said, "I only asked for the purple felt-tip—"

"No, I mean I've had ENOUGH of all this!" Kenny retorted, jumping to her feet. "All this Katie Shaw business has got well out of hand!"

"But there's nothing we can do about it," Fliss began.

"Oh, yes, there is." That glint was back in Kenny's eyes again. "Tomorrow morning I'm going to go straight up to Catherine Shaw, and I'm going to ask her for that disk back. And one way or another, I'm going to get it!"

CHAPTER SIX

"Kenny, are you sure this is a good idea?" I asked nervously.

It was the following morning, and we were in the playground, waiting for Catherine Shaw to arrive. I don't know about the others, but I, for one, was hoping that she wouldn't turn up at all.

"No, it isn't a *good* idea," Kenny replied, hopping from one foot to the other. She was really wound up. So would I be, if I had to face up to Catherine Shaw. "It's our *only* idea. That's why I've got to do it."

"Well, we can't let you go on your own,

Kenny," Frankie said firmly. "I think we should all come with you. What do you say, guys?"

Fliss and Rosie didn't look keen at all. Neither was I, but Frankie was right. We couldn't let Kenny do this on her own.

"Yeah, OK," I agreed. "After all, there's five of us and only one of her! Fliss?"

"All right," Fliss squeaked. "Rosie?"

"OK," Rosie muttered.

So now we were all in it together. And Catherine Shaw was coming through the playground gates *right at this very minute.*

"Here goes," Kenny said under her breath.

"Oh, don't go yet," Fliss mumbled, grabbing Kenny's arm. "Let's do it at breaktime."

"No, now," Kenny insisted. "Before we lose our nerve!"

We all trailed across the playground in Catherine's direction. She saw us coming, and glared at us.

"What do you lot want?" she asked, putting her arms protectively round her rucksack.

"OK, let's get down to business," Kenny

said coolly. "You've got our disk, and we want it back."

Catherine blinked. "What?"

"Our disk," Kenny repeated impatiently. "You've got it, we want it!"

Catherine looked completely blank. "I dunno what you're talking about," she complained. "What's a disk?"

"A *computer* disk," Frankie explained.

"I don't know anything about computers!" Catherine said, still looking bewildered.

"But you've got email," Kenny pointed out.

Catherine looked even more puzzled. "No I haven't."

My heart sank. It was pretty obvious that Catherine Shaw didn't have a clue what we were talking about. We'd lost our best suspect.

"Look, never mind," Frankie said quickly, and we all turned and walked off.

"Hey!" Catherine called after us angrily, as the penny finally dropped. "Are you calling me a thief?"

"Quick!" Rosie said urgently. "Leg it!"

We all raced off across the playground, and dashed into school.

"So that's that then," I said dismally, as we hung our coats up in the cloakroom. "We're still no closer to finding out who Katie Shaw is."

No-one said anything. It looked like we were *never* going to get the disk back.

"I still think it could be the M&Ms," said Fliss, for the millionth time.

"Or Ryan Scott and Danny McCloud," Frankie suggested.

"Maybe it *is* Catherine Shaw after all," Rosie suggested. "Maybe she just acted dumb to throw us off her trail."

It was Friday afternoon, and we were round at Frankie's place for our sleepover. Nothing much had happened since Tuesday, except that we were still getting an email every day from Katie Shaw, and every day the ransom money went up by a pound. It was now up to eleven quid.

We'd also finished designing the Aztec website, and we'd given all the stuff to Mr

Thomas. He was going to show us the site, which he'd nearly finished, when he got home from work later on.

"If we're going to get the disk back, it has to be this weekend," I said. We'd taken our shoes off, and we were all lying on the living-room floor in a row with our feet on the sofa. "Tom's finishing off his new design over the next few days, and he's taking it into school on Monday."

"Maybe we should give up then," Fliss suggested. "If Tom's got a new design, we don't need the disk anyway."

"Yeah, but the first design's the best one," I pointed out. "Tom's still gutted, and it's all our fault."

"We can't give up now anyway," Kenny said grimly. "I want to know who this Katie Shaw is. And boy, when I find out, she'll wish I hadn't!"

"Kenny, your feet stink!" Frankie complained.

"It's not me, it's Lyndz," Kenny said indignantly.

"Cheek!" I said. "These socks are brand-new."

"Yeah, but your *feet* aren't brand-new,

are they?" Kenny grinned.

We all started wiggling our feet about underneath each other's noses, and that made us giggle for a bit. But then we got all gloomy again.

"Do you think I should tell Tom we lost the disk?" I asked.

"What do you think he'll do?" Fliss asked anxiously.

"What, after he's killed me, you mean?" I replied.

"Honestly's the best policy, my gran always says," Frankie remarked.

"Nah, that's not right!" Kenny grabbed a cushion and tried to smother Frankie. "What you mean is, *honesty* – always gets you into trouble!"

We all grabbed a cushion then and had a cushion fight for ten minutes, until Frankie's mum came in and told us tea was ready. We were in the kitchen having cheese on toast, when Mr Thomas came home from work. He's a lawyer, remember? So is Frankie's mum, but she works from home more since she had Izzy.

"I've been working on your website all

week, girls," he beamed, sneaking a piece of Frankie's toast off her plate. "I think you're going to love it, even though I say so myself! Now, has your brother got any tapes of his band, Lyndz? I wouldn't mind hearing what they sound like."

"Oh, Dad!" Frankie grinned. "I don't think you'd be into that kind of music!"

"Why not?" Mr Thomas asked. "I was quite trendy in my day, I'll have you know, Francesca Thomas."

"*Dad*!" Frankie looked really embarrassed, but the rest of us couldn't help giggling. "No-one says *trendy* these days!"

"Well, hip, cool, funky or whatever it is." Mr Thomas winked at us. "So, do you want to see this website or not?"

Kenny snaffled the last piece of cheese on toast, and we all charged upstairs to Frankie's bedroom. Mr Thomas put the computer on, and we all waited impatiently while he found the website files.

"Right, just remember it's not finished yet," he warned us. "It'll look a lot better when I've spent some more time on it."

But although the website wasn't finished, it already looked pretty good to me when it opened up on the screen! We'd asked Mr Thomas to use purple, green and gold throughout the site, and it looked really fab. The photos of the band had come out well, too.

"I've still got to put in the rest of the stuff you gave me," Mr Thomas went on. "It's Tom's birthday next Saturday, isn't it, Lyndz? I'll have it finished by then."

"Thanks, Mr Thomas," I said gratefully, as he went out.

"Oh, Frankie," Mr Thomas popped his head round the door again. "I've got a document I need to work on tonight, so I'm going to be using the computer. So can you lot find something else to do for the rest of the evening?"

"Sure thing, Dad," Frankie agreed. She glanced at the rest of us. "I guess we'd better check our emails."

"What's the point?" Kenny grumbled. "There'll just be another one from that rat-faced old bag, Katie Shaw!"

"Maybe Barbie and the others have replied to our last message," Rosie pointed out. "We haven't heard from them for days."

Frankie found our site, and then checked the messages section. We had two new emails, one from Katie Shaw, which she deleted straight away, and another from the American girls.

Dear Frankie, Fliss, Kenny, Rosie and Lyndz

Sorry we haven't replied for ages, but we've been grounded for the last week. Our parents got mad when we had a pool party, and we accidentally soaked Barbie's nosey neighbour, Mrs Klein, with the sprinkler!

We were real sorry to hear about all the problems you're having with your mystery blackmailer. Why don't you set a trap for them like they do in the movies? You know, you say you'll pay them, then you go along to the meeting-place and bust 'em!

Let us know how you go.

Barbie, Darlene, Shannon and Jennie

Spooky Stories Music Shopping Midnight Feast Games

CHAPTER SEVEN

We all stared at each other.

"That's a totally wicked idea!" Kenny gasped. "Why didn't *we* think of that?"

"Quick, Frankie," Rosie said urgently. "Write an email to Katie Shaw, telling her we'll meet her tomorrow – with the money!"

"We're not really going to give her the money, are we?" Fliss asked.

"'Course not, birdbrain," Kenny replied. "But Katie Shaw will have to arrange somewhere for us to leave the cash, then we'll hide ourselves away and pounce on her!"

81

"Not if it's Catherine Shaw, we won't!" Fliss muttered.

Frankie was typing away furiously.

OK, you win. We've decided to pay up. We want the disk back tomorrow, so you'll have to tell us where and when we can meet.
The Sleepover Club

"There!" Frankie sent the email. "That should do the trick. Now all we've got to do is wait for Katie Shaw to reply."

Mr Thomas stuck his head round the door again. "Frankie, I need to use the computer *now*," he warned her.

"OK, Dad, it's all yours." Frankie logged out of our site, and we all trooped downstairs again. "What do you guys want to do now?"

"What about Robot Wars?" Kenny suggested, bumping into Fliss and locking her arms round her. Our Robot Wars game had kind of taken over from International Gladiators, but it was still really rough! We all pretended to be robots with different

powers, and we had to try and knock each other out of the arena, which was usually a circle of cushions. It was ace fun!

"Nah, let's play Cluedo," Rosie suggested. "We haven't played that for ages."

"OK," Kenny agreed. "I feel like murdering someone!"

We all sat down on the living-room floor, and Frankie went to get the Cluedo box. We set up the board and dealt out the cards.

"I wonder if Katie Shaw's replied yet," Kenny said. "I think it's Professor Plum in the conservatory with the dagger."

Fliss, who was next, wasn't listening.

"Fliss!" Kenny gave her a nudge, and got a good look at her cards at the same time. "Professor Plum, conservatory, dagger."

"Sorry." Fliss looked flustered. "I was just wondering if Katie Shaw has replied yet. Hang on a minute, Kenny."

"Don't bother," Kenny said breezily. "I saw all your cards anyway!"

"That's not fair!" Fliss moaned, picking up the dice. She moved her piece into the study. "I think it's Katie Shaw, in the study with the

revolver. I mean, Miss Scarlett, not Katie Shaw!"

"Oh, this is hopeless!" Frankie threw down her cards. "None of us can concentrate. Let's nip upstairs and ask my dad if we can check the email."

Mr Thomas didn't look that pleased to see us when we thundered into Frankie's bedroom like a herd of baby elephants, but he agreed to let us check the emails, if we were really quick. We were disappointed, though. Katie Shaw hadn't replied.

We went back downstairs, and finished the Cluedo game. Kenny won – she guessed that it was Mrs White in the study with the lead piping. Then Frankie got out Pictionary and we played that for a bit.

"It's been ages since we last checked the email," Rosie said. "Katie Shaw might have replied by now."

We all looked at Frankie.

"Oh, *all right*," Frankie agreed. "But my dad's not going to be too pleased."

This time we tiptoed upstairs, and stuck our heads round the door. Mr Thomas didn't

even notice us. He had his head bent over the computer, typing away furiously. The document he was working on looked pretty boring and complicated.

"Hi, Dad," Frankie said sweetly. But Mr Thomas didn't even turn round.

"Sorry, girls, I've got to get this done," he said.

"But, Dad—" Frankie began.

"You can use the computer tomorrow," her dad said firmly, still typing.

"Tomorrow!" Fliss grumbled, as we went downstairs again. "What if Katie Shaw's replied? We won't even know."

"Yeah, say if she wants to meet us really early in the morning?" Rosie pointed out. "If we don't read the email tonight, we might miss the meeting."

"We could put the computer on when we're supposed to be in bed tonight," Kenny suggested, glancing at Frankie.

Frankie's parents have this really strict rule that the computer is *never* put on after we've been sent to bed. When they first got the Internet, they had this password which

Frankie didn't know, so that she couldn't get on the Net without them being there. But then Fliss found out the password, when we were doing our Vikings project for school, and ever since then, Mr and Mrs Thomas have let Frankie use it whenever she wants – but *not* when she's supposed to be asleep.

Frankie looked a bit uncomfortable. "My parents'll go mad if they find out," she muttered. "They won't let me use the computer for *weeks*."

"So we'll make sure they *don't* find out!" Kenny urged her. "Come on, Franks, don't you want to see if Katie Shaw's replied yet or not?"

"Well, OK," Frankie agreed. "But we've got to be really quiet. And no messing about."

"Would we ever!" Kenny snorted. "Nothing's gonna go wrong, Frankie. Trust me."

"We may have been best mates since we were little kids, Kenz, but I'm not *that* crazy!" Frankie retorted.

Mr Thomas was just finishing off his document when we went up to Frankie's bedroom to get our pyjamas and toothbrushes.

"OK, girls, I'll get out of your way now," he yawned. "And you remember the rules, don't you?" He eyeballed us sternly. "No computers after lights out. Right?"

"Right!" we all agreed innocently.

There was the usual scramble for the bathroom, and we were in there for a while because Kenny started a wet flannel fight. But we were all tucked up in bed, looking as if butter wouldn't melt in our mouths, when Frankie's mum came in to turn off the light. I was sharing with Frankie, Fliss and Rosie were in the bunk beds and Kenny was on the pull-down bed in her sleeping bag.

"Night night, girls." Mrs Thomas switched off the light. "And don't let the bedbugs bite!"

We lay there and counted up to twenty, then we all reached for our torches and switched them on.

"Shall we have our midnight feast first?" Kenny asked, rubbing her tum. "I'm starving."

"No, let's check the emails first," Frankie whispered. "I'm too wound up to eat anything until we've got that over with!"

We all climbed out of bed, and tiptoed over to the computer. Rosie rolled up her jumper and put it across the bottom of the bedroom door, so that the light from the computer screen didn't shine out on to the landing. Then Frankie switched the machine on. The *click* sounded deafening, and we all held our breaths for a minute. But no-one came bursting in, yelling at us.

"Come on, come on," Frankie muttered under her breath as we waited for our site to load. She was really jittery. So were the rest of us. We all watched silently as our Home Page opened up on the screen, and Frankie checked the messages.

"Look, Katie Shaw's replied!" Kenny said triumphantly, and then immediately clapped her hand over her mouth.

"SSSHHH!" we all hissed. We probably made more noise than Kenny did!

Frankie opened up the email, and we all crowded round to read it.

So you've finally decided to see sense! This is what you've got to do. Wrap eleven pounds up in a plastic bag, and

leave it in the park tomorrow morning, under the hedge behind the swings. The package must be there by 10 o'clock on the dot, or you won't get the disk. The disk will be returned to you when I've got the money.

"What a cheek!" Kenny whispered, clenching her fists. "You wait – we'll be ready for her tomorrow!"

"Hang on a minute," I said. "Are we going to pretend we've left the money, before we hide and try to catch her?"

"Yeah, good idea," Frankie said. "Katie Shaw might be hiding and watching *us*, waiting to see if we leave the money where she said."

"OK, we need to make up a dummy package then!" Kenny said gleefully. "What can we use?"

"We could use a bit of paper, folded up," Fliss suggested. "That would feel like a five-pound note."

"I've got some plastic coins somewhere," Frankie said. "From years ago when I used to play Shops. I think it's in a box in the garage."

"Excellent!" Kenny rubbed her hands together. "Maybe you'd better send a reply,

Frankie. Just to let Katie Shaw know that we've got her email."

Frankie sent a reply, and gave a sigh of relief. "OK, now we can have our midnight feast!"

"I can't wait to see who Katie Shaw is tomorrow," Rosie said, as Frankie logged off the Internet. "Do you really think it's someone we know?"

"Sure to be," Kenny said grimly. "Like Frankie said, they could just be hiding behind someone else's email address."

"What was that?" Fliss squeaked suddenly.

We all froze. It sounded like a bedroom door opening, followed by footsteps across the landing. And Frankie was still closing the computer down!

We all panicked. Frankie started trying to hit all the buttons as fast as possible. Me and Rosie both jumped backwards, and bumped heads, and Kenny tried to leap over to her bed, and banged straight into Fliss, who went flying and ended up sprawled over the computer keyboard.

"Fliss!" Frankie hissed frantically, trying to push her off. "Get out of the way!"

I don't know how we managed it, but somehow we got ourselves into bed and under the covers in about ten seconds flat. Frankie was last, because she had to switch the computer off. She just about had time to dive under the duvet and close her eyes before the door opened softly, and Mrs Thomas looked in.

"Phew! That was close!" Kenny whispered, as we heard Frankie's mum go into the bathroom.

"Never mind, at least we didn't get caught," Rosie said cheerfully. "I've got some Milky Way Stars. Does anyone want one?"

Fliss, Kenny and me started pulling our midnight feast stuff out of our bags too. But Frankie was sitting up in bed, frowning.

"What's the matter, Franks?" Kenny asked, biting into a king-size Snickers bar. "Look, everything's sorted now, and your mum didn't know we were on the computer. It's cool."

"No, it isn't," Frankie said in this kind of strangled voice.

"Why not?" I asked.

"You know my dad's document, the one he was working on?" Frankie looked even more worried. "Well, I saw it when I was closing the computer down. But then Fliss fell on the keyboard – and I didn't see the document then after that."

"What?" Kenny stared at her. "You don't mean – Fliss accidentally *deleted* it?"

"I couldn't have done!" Fliss was aghast.

"Maybe the document was still there, and you just didn't notice because you were panicking about your mum coming in," Rosie suggested.

"Perhaps we should check the computer again, just to make sure," I said.

Frankie nodded, and climbed out of bed. She turned the computer on, and we all stood there waiting for it to fire up.

"See all those little symbols?" Frankie pointed at the screen. "Well, there was one there to click on which was called *Work Document*. That was Dad's stuff. And now it's gone."

Spooky Stories   Music   Shopping   Midnight Feast   Games

CHAPTER EIGHT

We couldn't believe it. We'd only gone and deleted the document that Frankie's dad had been working so hard on all evening.

"I think the Sleepover Club is jinxed when it comes to computers!" Rosie said miserably.

"It's all your fault, Fliss," Kenny moaned. "If you hadn't fallen on the keyboard, this would never have happened!"

"Well, you're the one who pushed me!" Fliss retorted. "And anyway, you started all this by losing Tom's disk."

"Look, let's not argue," I said quickly,

trying to calm things down. "We've got to decide what we're going to do."

"What do you mean?" Frankie asked. "We've deleted the document, and that's it. It's gone."

"Maybe we could type it up again," Rosie suggested.

"Yes, great idea!" Kenny said eagerly. "Frankie, do you know which document it was?"

"I suppose it's the one that Dad left lying on the dining-room table," Frankie said doubtfully.

"All right, you go and get it then," Kenny replied, "and we'll take turns at typing it up."

Frankie tiptoed over to the door. "Come with me, Lyndz," she whispered.

"OK." I followed her out of the bedroom, and on to the landing. Mr and Mrs Thomas's bedroom light was off by now, so it was really dark out there.

"Hold my hand, Lyndz," Frankie whispered. "I can find my way around, no problem – *ouch*!"

"Are you OK?" I asked.

"I stubbed my toe on the banister!" Frankie groaned. "Come on, once we get down the stairs a bit, I'll put my torch on."

We hurried downstairs and into the dining room. A red folder was lying on the table.

"I think that's it," Frankie whispered.

I picked up the folder and took a look. It was a legal document, so I couldn't understand a word. It was full of really old-fashioned language, and my eyes nearly popped out of my head when I saw how long it was.

"Frankie, this is enormous!" I hissed. "It's going to take us all night to copy this!"

"I know," she said grimly.

The others nearly fainted with shock when we took the document back upstairs. But we didn't have any choice. We just had to get on with it. Frankie created a new file with the same name as before, and she offered to do the first few pages. Meanwhile, the rest of us were yawning like mad, so we crawled into bed to get a bit of sleep.

It seemed like I'd only just closed my

eyes when Frankie was shaking me by the shoulder.

"Lyndz, it's your turn," she yawned. "Wake Kenny up next."

I could hardly keep my eyes open as I sat down at the computer. Frankie snuggled down into bed, and I started typing. It wouldn't have been so bad if I'd understood what I was doing, but the document was so complicated, I didn't have a clue what it was about! I struggled on for the next hour, and then shook Kenny awake.

"Eh? Wassup?" Kenny mumbled, her eyes still firmly closed.

"It's your turn to type, Kenny!" I said. Then I jumped into bed, and was asleep just about the moment my head hit the pillow...

"Lyndz! Wake up!"

Someone was shaking me again, and I didn't want to wake up this time. I'd already got up twice more during the night to take my turn at typing the document again, and now I wasn't getting up for anybody!

"Lyndz! Wake up!" Frankie pulled the duvet

off me. "It's ten past nine! We've only got a little while before we meet Katie Shaw."

"Yikes!" I gasped. I forced myself to sit up, and rub my eyes. They felt really heavy and sore. I looked blearily round at the others, who were rolling reluctantly out of bed too. They didn't look any better than I felt.

"Did we finish the document?" I asked anxiously.

Frankie nodded. "I finished it off at three in the morning," she said, "And I spellchecked it too."

"I bet there were loads of spelling mistakes," Rosie said with a grin. "I was so tired, I didn't even know what I was typing!"

The door opened, and Mrs Thomas looked in. She was carrying Izzy.

"Goodness me, I thought you were never going to get up!" she said. "Breakfast's ready, so hurry up and get washed and dressed. Your dad wants to come in and print out his document."

We all glanced at each other.

"Let's hope he doesn't notice anything funny," Fliss said.

"He won't," Frankie said confidently. "We did a great job!"

"Have we got time for breakfast?" Kenny asked in a low voice.

"Just about," Frankie replied. "Anyway, my mum'll get suspicious if we shoot off without eating."

We didn't bother with washing. We just got dressed and raced downstairs. We were scoffing the pancakes and maple syrup that Mrs Thomas had made, when we heard Frankie's dad coming down the stairs. He came into the kitchen, looking rather peculiar.

"I think there's something wrong with that computer," he said, looking puzzled. "You know that document I typed up last night?"

Frankie's mum nodded, while we just all looked down at our plates.

"Well, I've just printed it off," Mrs Thomas went on, holding up a pile of papers, "and it's a *different* document to the one I typed up last night!" He stared round at us. "Anyone like to tell me how that happened?"

We all looked pretty embarrassed, and started squirming in our seats.

"Sorry, Dad," Frankie muttered. "We kind of deleted your document by accident…"

Mrs Thomas raised her eyebrows. "That must have been difficult," she remarked, "seeing that you're not allowed on the computer after lights out."

"We *were* on the computer after lights out," Kenny muttered. "Sorry, Mrs Thomas."

"So you thought you'd type up my document again, only it was the wrong one!" Frankie's dad said sternly.

This was *awful*! We were in REAL trouble this time. I was so worried that it took a few seconds before Mr Thomas's next words sank in.

"Good job I can get my proper document back again!"

"WHAT?" we all yelled with relief. "How?"

"You click on the symbol labelled Recycle Bin." Frankie's dad actually looked as if he was trying not to smile. "Documents which have been deleted always hang around in

there for a while, in case you change your mind and want them back."

"Frankie! You idiot!" Kenny said crossly.

"Well, how was I supposed to know?" Frankie defended herself. "I'm not a computer expert!"

"I'm not very happy with you at all, Francesca," said Mrs Thomas coolly, and we knew that we were in for a real roasting.

We all had to sit there then and listen to Frankie's mum and dad going on and on about how we'd betrayed their trust, and really let them down. I don't know how the others took it, but I felt pretty bad. Frankie was banned from using the computer for two weeks, and they said if she did it again, she wouldn't be allowed to have it in her room any more. They calmed down a bit when we hinted that the reason we'd been using the computer was something to do with Tom's birthday website, and that we weren't just messing around, but they were still pretty mad.

Meanwhile, we were all glancing anxiously at the clock every few minutes. It was now

quarter to ten, and we hadn't even made up the dummy package yet. Finally, Mr and Mrs Thomas thought that they'd told us off enough, and they let us go.

It was ten to ten when we dashed into the living room. Kenny quickly folded up a small piece of paper, while Rosie fetched the plastic bag her midnight feast stuff had been wrapped in, and Frankie nipped out to the garage to find the fake coins. She was *ages*.

"Where is she?" Kenny muttered. She was so impatient, steam was nearly coming out of her ears! "We're going to be late!"

Just then Frankie dashed in again. "Sorry, it wasn't where I thought it was!" she panted. "But I found it in the end."

Quickly we put the folded piece of paper and the plastic coins into the carrier bag, and knotted the top tightly. Then we ran out of the house, and down the road.

"It's nearly ten o'clock!" Rosie gasped, looking at her watch as we dashed through Cuddington. "Do you think Katie Shaw will wait for us?"

"Dunno," Kenny panted. "Just keep running!"

We got to the park at just after five past ten. We were all so tired, we could hardly even limp across the play area to where the swings were.

"I can see something under the hedge!" Frankie said eagerly, as we made our way over to it.

"It's probably just a bit of litter," Kenny replied.

But it wasn't. It was a note. And it wasn't a very nice note either.

YOU WERE TOLD TO BE HERE AT 10 O'CLOCK, AND YOU WEREN'T. YOU'D BETTER HAVE A REALLY GOOD EXCUSE, OR YOU'RE GOING TO BE IN BIG TROUBLE...

CHAPTER NINE

"Oh, rats!" Kenny groaned furiously, ripping the note into tiny shreds. "Katie Shaw was here – and we missed her!"

"We were only a few minutes late as well," Fliss wheezed, clinging on to Rosie for support. We were all huffing and puffing and panting as if we'd just run the London Marathon.

"Hang on a minute." Frankie shaded her eyes, and looked round the play area. "Fliss is right – we *were* only a few minutes late."

"So?" I said.

"Well, maybe Katie Shaw's still here,"

103

Frankie suggested. "In the park, I mean."

"What!" Kenny clenched her fists. "Do you really think she might be?"

"Well, we know she was here about five minutes ago, because she left the note for us," Frankie pointed out. "She could still be close by."

We all stared around the play area. It was pretty empty because it was still quite early, and there was only a mum with her toddler, who was playing in the sandpit.

"I don't think it's them, do you?" Rosie grinned.

"Let's take a look around the rest of the park," Kenny suggested. She looked really wound up by now – Katie Shaw was in for a right earful if we ever caught up with her!

We left the play area, and walked across the grass towards the football field. We were just going past the ice-cream stand, which was closed, when Frankie clutched my arm.

"Look!" she hissed.

We could hardly believe our eyes. The M&Ms were walking along the path ahead of us, arm in arm!

"It's them!" Kenny hissed furiously. "It's the Queen and the Goblin – *they're* Katie Shaw!"

"And they've probably got the disk on them right now," I whispered.

"Quick, after them!" Frankie said.

"I'm gonna push both of them into the duckpond!" Kenny said under her breath, as we began to run towards them. "Don't try to stop me, anybody!"

"Hang on a minute." Rosie had stopped dead, while the rest of us were still running.

"Come on, Rosie-Posie, or we might lose them!" Kenny yelled impatiently over her shoulder. In the distance we could see the M&Ms heading towards the park gate.

"Look!" Rosie beckoned us to come back, and pointed over at the football field. Two very familiar figures were knocking a football around. It was Ryan Scott and Danny McCloud!

"What are they doing here?" Kenny gasped.

"I dunno," Rosie wailed, "but it could be them, couldn't it? *They* could be Katie Shaw!"

105

We all groaned. It was pretty bad luck to see *two* of our best suspects at the same time. What were we supposed to do now?

"Me and Fliss'll go after the M&Ms," Kenny decided quickly. "And Frankie, you and Rosie and Lyndz go after Ryan and Danny."

Fliss pouted. "Why can't I stay with Frankie and the others?" she asked.

"Because you'll turn to jelly if Ryan smiles at you!" Kenny said, grabbing her hand. "Come on!"

"Hold on a minute." Frankie was staring through the railings at the street outside the park. "Who's *that*?"

We all stared. Would you believe it, Catherine Shaw was walking along the pavement, eating a Wispa bar!

"Oh no!" Kenny slapped her forehead. "They're *all* here!"

"What are we going to do now?" Frankie asked. "We can't accuse them *all* of being Katie Shaw."

"Maybe we should just send an email to her saying we want to set up another meeting," Rosie suggested.

"Yeah, we could make it this afternoon," Fliss said.

"And we can still try and catch them red-handed," I added. "Then Tom will get his disk back in time to do the posters for the gig."

"Good idea," Kenny agreed. "Let's go back to my place – it's closest."

We all trailed out of the park, and headed for the McKenzie house. It was pretty frustrating to know that *one* of our suspects might even have had the disk on them when we saw them a few minutes ago. But Frankie was right. We couldn't go around accusing everyone of being Katie Shaw. Not unless we had some proof anyway.

Kenny's mum let us in when we rang the doorbell.

"Did you have a good sleepover, girls?" she asked, then took a closer look at us. "My goodness, you look like you were up all night!"

"Don't be silly, Mum," Kenny said, trying to smother this absolutely enormous yawn. Of course, that set us all off yawning then.

"Yes, I can see you all look bright-eyed and bushy-tailed," Mrs McKenzie said, raising her eyebrows.

"Mum, is it all right if we use the computer?" Kenny asked quickly, before Mrs M had time to ask any more awkward questions.

Her mum nodded. "Your dad's out on an emergency call, so there's no-one in the study. And Molly's out with Louise."

"Good," Kenny muttered, as we headed for her dad's study. "We don't want Molly the Monster finding out what's going on – we'd never hear the end of it!"

Kenny's dad's a doctor, so the study's full of all these gruesome charts and medical books. He's even got a *skeleton* in there!

"That's what Katie Shaw's going to look like when I've finished with her!" Kenny joked, nodding at the skeleton as she switched the computer on.

"What shall we put in the email?" Rosie asked.

"We'll just say that we couldn't help being late, and we really want to arrange another meeting," Frankie said.

"What's the matter, Kenny?" Fliss wanted to know. Kenny had logged on to our site, and was staring at the messages section.

"We've got a new message from Katie Shaw!" she said, looking puzzled.

"What?" I frowned. "That was quick, seeing as we've only just got back from the park ourselves."

"Maybe she sent it *before* she left for the park this morning," Rosie suggested.

"Quick, open it up, Kenny, and have a look," Frankie urged her. "The email will have the time it was sent on it."

Kenny clicked on the email.

"It was sent at ten-fifteen this morning," she told us, pointing at the time and the date.

"But we were in the park until ten past ten, and so were the others," Frankie pointed out. "How could *any* of them have got back in time to send this email at ten-fifteen?"

"Emma Hughes lives quite close to the park," Kenny said doubtfully. "But I dunno if she'd have had time to get home, put the computer on and send an email, all in five minutes."

"What about Ryan and Danny?" Rosie asked.

"Ryan lives in Stamford Close," Fliss piped up, then blushed as we all turned to look at her. "I just happen to remember that," she said hastily.

"And Danny lives near me," I said. "I don't know where Catherine Shaw lives."

Frankie was staring at the screen, her eyes almost popping out of her head. "Have you read the email?" she asked.

You weren't on time this morning, so the price goes up again. Now it's DOUBLED! If you want the disk back, it's going to cost you twenty-two pounds. And if you don't pay up, I'll give the disk back to Tom Collins, and tell him EXACTLY how you lost it!

We were all fuming, especially Kenny.

"I'm totally fed up with this!" she yelled.

"Let's just write back and tell her to get lost," Rosie suggested. "After all, Tom's doing a new poster, and we don't need all this hassle."

"Yeah, but then we won't find out who it

is," Frankie pointed out. "Not unless we arrange another meeting."

"But what if Katie Shaw goes and tells Tom what happened?" I said anxiously. "I'm going to be in doom forever. And my parents are going to kill me – if Tom doesn't first!"

"I think we should stick to our original plan," Fliss said. "I think we should go along and pretend to leave the money, and then find out who it is."

"I'm with Rosie," Kenny grumbled. "Even if we try and catch her, how do we know it'll work? She might be so mad that we've left fake money, she'll just go and tell Tom anyway."

"Maybe I should just confess to Tom right now," I said. "Then we *can* tell Katie Shaw to get lost."

We just didn't know *what* to do. There were so many things to think about, our heads were spinning.

"Look, don't reply to that email yet, Kenny," Frankie said. "Not until we've decided what we're going to do."

"OK," Kenny replied, switching the computer off. "Let's go up to my room, and we can talk about it."

We all trailed gloomily out of the study, and up the stairs. Molly the Monster was at her friend's so we had the room to ourselves.

"I'm sick of Molly's mess," Kenny said, picking a huge heap of clothes off the floor, and dumping them on Molly's bed. "Honestly, if it wasn't for her, this room would be really tidy."

"Oh, yeah?" Frankie raised her eyebrows as she stepped over a pair of Kenny's trainers lying in the middle of the floor on top of a pair of jeans.

"So what are we going to do?" I asked. "About Katie Shaw?"

"We either tell her to get lost or we try and catch her," Rosie said. "That seems to be pretty much it."

"Yeah, and I reckon she's had enough fun with us," Kenny said grimly. "It's about time we put a stop to it!"

"Don't you want to know who it is, Kenny?" Frankie asked.

"'Course I do," Kenny shrugged. "But even if we find out who it is, she might still drop us right in it with Tom."

"I don't want *that* if I can help it," I added. "*Hic!*"

"Now look what you've done," Frankie said to Kenny. "You've given Lyndz hiccups."

"Sorry – *hic!*" I gulped. "It's just that I'm really stressed out."

"Hold your breath, Lyndz," Fliss said, as Frankie started hunting around for something cold to put down my back.

The front door slammed, and there was the sound of footsteps running up the stairs. A moment later, Molly and her friend Louise came into the bedroom.

"Oh, not you lot again," Molly sniffed. "Well, you can get out of here, NOW. Me and Louise have got homework to do."

"Go into the study then." Kenny glared at her. The mood she was in, you could see that she was ready for a fight! "We were here first."

"*Hic!*" I said again, and clapped my hand over my mouth.

113

"Do you mind *not* hiccuping your horrible germs all over my bedroom?" Molly said, and she and Louise sniggered.

"You leave Lyndz alone," Kenny scowled, as Molly picked up her schoolbag and began pulling books out of it.

"*Hic!*" I got up and started walking around the room, trying to hold my breath. Suddenly Frankie came up behind me and slapped me on the back, hard. I wasn't expecting it at all. I stumbled forward, and banged straight into Louise, who wasn't expecting it either. *She* stumbled forward, and bumped straight into Molly's bedside table. All the stuff on it flew off, including the bedside light, an empty glass and a little wooden box, painted with flowers.

"You stupid idiot, Lyndz!" Molly yelled, red-faced. "Look what you've done!"

"Sorry, Lyndz," Frankie apologised. "I thought if I took you by surprise, it might cure your hiccups!"

"It did," I said, but I wasn't bothered about that now. I was staring down at the carpet.

The lid of the little wooden box had flown off when it hit the floor, and a computer disk had fallen out.

It was labelled:

INDEX

Very important!

Property of Tom Collins

CHAPTER TEN

There was silence in the room for about thirty seconds. Molly and Louise both turned a very deep red, and started shuffling their feet.

"The disk," Kenny said faintly. She charged across the room and picked it up. "It is!" she said more loudly. "It's Tom's disk!"

She swivelled round, and glared at Molly and Louise. "It was *you*. You're Katie Shaw!"

"So?" Molly jeered, obviously trying to make the best of it. "You lot are so stupid, you didn't even *know* we had the disk. We had it right from the start. You dropped it

116

here when you came round after the sleepover at Lyndz's— OW!"

Kenny had lunged forward and given Molly a shove. She cannoned into Louise, and the two of them went flying on to the bed.

"Let me at them!" Kenny yelled, launching herself forward, but luckily Frankie and Rosie grabbed her arms and dragged her off.

"We really had you fooled," Molly went on scornfully. "Didn't we, Louise?"

"Yeah, we did," Louise muttered in this weedy little voice. You could tell she was dead scared of Kenny!

"You knew that disk belonged to Tom," Kenny roared. Her voice was muffled because Frankie and Rosie were pinning her to the bed, not letting her move. "You had no right to keep it!"

Suddenly the door opened.

"What on earth's going on here?" Mrs McKenzie was standing there, frowning.

I glanced at Molly and Louise. They both looked pretty nervous, and that gave me an idea.

"Nothing, Mrs McKenzie," Frankie said. "Just Molly and Kenny fighting, as usual."

"You two!" Kenny's mum sighed. "I don't know why you can't just get on with each other." And she went out, shutting the door behind her.

"You're just mad because we fooled you," Molly taunted Kenny. "We win!"

"No, you don't," Fliss said hotly, "because we've got the disk back, and we haven't paid you a penny. So there!"

"Yeah, Fliss is right." Kenny looked a bit brighter. "You lose!"

Molly looked incredibly smug. "Not when we tell Tom Collins that *you* were the ones who nicked his disk!"

"You wouldn't!" Kenny said, dismayed.

Molly grinned. "Watch me."

I stepped forward into the middle of the room. "In that case, there's only one thing we can do, Kenny," I said. "I think we should go downstairs right away and tell your mum exactly what's happened."

This time it was Molly and Louise's turn to look shocked.

"Lyndz! What are you talking about?" Kenny began, but I interrupted her.

"And then I think we should go and confess to Tom, and tell *him* exactly what happened," I went on.

I could see that Frankie and the others were beginning to catch on, but Kenny was still too wound up to see where I was heading.

"I don't get it, Lyndz," she said crossly. "We'll just get into a whole heap of trouble if we do that!"

"Well, Tom might be a bit upset at first," I admitted. "But once we explain that we took the disk for a special surprise for his birthday, I think he'll forgive us." I stared hard at Molly the Monster and Louise, who were beginning to look very uncomfortable. "I reckon he'll be *much* more annoyed with the people who found the disk and didn't give it back!"

Kenny began to grin. "Yeah, you're right, Lyndz!"

"And I don't suppose your mum and dad would be too pleased if they knew Molly had

tried to blackmail us," I went on, playing my last and best card. "So, actually, I don't think we'll get into any trouble anyway. But I think Molly and Louise probably will!"

Louise glared at Molly. "I *told* you we shouldn't have done all that," she squeaked. "My sister'll go mad if she finds out I've been using her email address!"

"You're bluffing." Molly stared straight back at me. "You wouldn't go and tell my mum."

I grinned. "Watch me!"

There was silence for a minute.

"OK," Molly said through gritted teeth at last. "You don't tell Mum and Dad, and we won't tell Tom you took his disk."

I looked at the others. "Deal?" I asked.

"Deal!" said Kenny, grinning all over her face. "*Now* who loses?"

Molly and Louise didn't answer. Still red in the face, they flounced out of the room, and we heard them stomping off down the stairs. Then we all started laughing and doing high fives.

"That showed *them*!" Frankie grinned.

"It all makes sense now," Kenny said. "Louise Ball lives right next to the park – that's how they got back to her house so quickly to send the email. We must have just missed them. And I knew Louise had a sister who's married – I just didn't know her name was Katie Shaw."

"You were so smart, Lyndz!" Rosie said admiringly. "You really showed Molly the Monster who's boss."

"Yeah, Lyndz, I didn't know you could be so devious!" And Kenny slapped me on the back. "Oops!" she added, as the disk flew out of her hand and landed on the carpet.

"I think I'll look after that from now on!" I said, picking it up. "And the first thing I'm going to do is give it back to Tom. Let's go round to my place."

"No, the first thing we're going to do is copy the poster for the website," Frankie said.

"OK," I agreed. "But I'm not letting this disk out of my sight, until it's safely back with Tom!"

* * *

121

"It's my disk!"

Tom stared down at it, looking completely dazed as if he couldn't believe his eyes. "Where did you get it?"

"Kenny found it," I said. "It must have fallen into her sleepover bag by accident." That was the story we'd agreed on.

"I'm really sorry, Tom," Kenny added.

"No worries," Tom said, still gazing at the disk as if he thought it was going to vanish into thin air or something. "Oh, this is cool. Now I can get the posters out on Monday. Thanks, girls."

We slipped out of his bedroom, and grinned at each other.

"I know it's not my turn, but can we have our sleepover here next Friday night?" I asked the others. "I really want you to be here when I show Tom the Aztec website."

"Sure, no problem," everyone agreed.

"Hey, aren't the band playing at the comp that Friday night?" Rosie asked.

I nodded.

"Wouldn't it be great if we could go along and see them?" Fliss suggested.

Well, everyone went wild at that idea, so of course, I had to go and ask my dad, didn't I? He wasn't sure at first, but we all promised to be really good and not get in the way. In the end he said he could sneak us backstage so that we could see the gig, but then we had to go straight home. Cool or what?

So there we all were on Friday night, crammed in backstage at the school hall, watching Tom and his band playing a whole load of songs at the disco. We even managed to have a dance, although Kenny's attempt at break-dancing wasn't too successful – she nearly broke one of the stage lights!

It was really weird to see *my brother* on stage being a popstar, but it was great too. Everyone seemed to like them – they clapped and cheered for more, which was a bit awkward because the band only have about six songs, so they had to sing some of them again.

We were having a great time, so we didn't really want to go home when Dad came to fetch us. But we'd promised to go without a fuss, so we all went back to my place and got

into our jim-jams, and my mum made us some hot chocolate. Then we went up to bed, and had our midnight feast. Tom didn't get back till after twelve, because the disco went on quite late, but we were still up, waiting for him. When we heard him come into the house, we rushed into his bedroom and put the computer on. Quickly we linked up to the Internet, and found the Aztec website. Frankie's dad had put it on the Net that morning.

"Happy birthday!" we all chorused, as Tom walked into the room.

Tom blinked. "Hey, I thought you lot'd be asleep ages ago," he grinned. "Did you enjoy the gig?" Then he spotted the computer screen and blinked again. "What's that?"

"Your birthday present," I said proudly. "And it's after midnight now, so it really is your birthday!"

The website looked so great. Mr Thomas had done everything we asked him to, and where he'd changed things, he'd made them better. Everything was on there: the info about the band, the photos, the horoscopes

page and the list of songs, as well as the poster.

"Do you like it?" I asked anxiously, as Tom scrolled through the pages.

"Lyndz, it's brilliant!" he said, shaking his head as if he couldn't believe it. "It's the best present I've ever had!"

"That's lucky," Kenny whispered in my ear, "after all the hassle we had!"

Well, that's about it for now. Everything turned out OK, and we didn't even get into any big trouble this time round. Cool or what?

Well, *we* didn't get into any trouble, but our American friends Darlene, Barbie, Jennie and Shannon did. Shannon's mum was showing her clown ornament to a friend, when its hat fell off and hit her on the toe! Now Shannon and the others have been grounded, and told they can't have any more sleepovers. So they've emailed us asking how they can change their parents' minds. We'll be able to give them loads of advice – after all, we're experts at getting ourselves into trouble, and experts at getting ourselves *out* of it too!

See ya soon!

45

Sleepover Girls Go Dancing

Hand jive, mashed potato – are you ready to groove? The Sleepover Club gets dance fever when the British National Ballet comes to Cuddington and announces a dance competition. They've got the moves, they've even got the music, they've even got the costumes. Go, S Club 5!

Pack up your sleepover kit and shimmy on over!

Collins

www.fireandwater.com
Visit the book lover's website

Order Form

To order direct from the publishers, just make a list of the titles you want and fill in the form below:

Name ....

Address ....

....

....

Send to: Dept 6, HarperCollins Publishers Ltd, Westerhill Road, Bishopbriggs, Glasgow G64 2QT.

Please enclose a cheque or postal order to the value of the cover price, plus:

UK & BFPO: Add £1.00 for the first book, and 25p per copy for each additional book ordered.

Overseas and Eire: Add £2.95 service charge. Books will be sent by surface mail but quotes for airmail despatch will be given on request.

A 24-hour telephone ordering service is available to holders of Visa, MasterCard, Amex or Switch cards on 0141- 772 2281.

Collins
An *Imprint* of HarperCollins*Publishers*

Have you been invited to all these sleepovers?

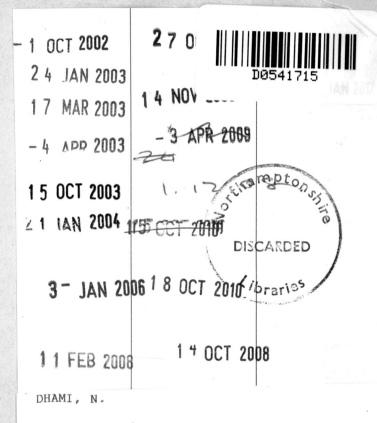

- 1 OCT 2002   2 7 0

2 4 JAN 2003

1 7 MAR 2003   1 4 NOV ....

- 4 APR 2003   - 3 APR 2009

15 OCT 2003

2 1 IAN 2004   1 5 OCT 2010

3 - JAN 2006 1 8 OCT 2010

Northamptonshire
DISCARDED
Libraries

1 1 FEB 2008   1 4 OCT 2008

D0541715

DHAMI, N.

sleepoverclub.com

Please return or renew this item by the last date shown.
You may renew items (unless they have been requested
by another customer) by telephoning, writing to or calling
in at any library.   100% recycled paper   *BKS 1 (5/95)*

80 001 784 492

Sch